THE
MAGIC SHOW
FROM THE
BLACK LAGOON®

THE
MAGIC SHOW
FROM THE
BLACK LAGOON®

by Mike Thaler
Illustrated by Jared Lee

SCHOLASTIC INC.

For Patty, my wife.
The magic of my life.
—M.T.

To classmate Judy Swagger Fetters.
—J.L.

CAT DISAPPEARED

Text copyright © 2020 by Mike Thaler
Illustrations copyright © 2020 by Jared Lee

ISBN 978-1-338-63049-7

10 9 8 7 6 5 4 3 2 1   20 21 22 23 24

Printed in the U.S.A.   40
First printing 2020

POUTING POSSUM →

CONTENTS

MAGIC WAND ←

JUST A STICK →

CHAPTER 1
A STAR IS BORN

"Pick a card," says Eric, holding out one card to me. "Look at it."

"It's the Queen of Hearts," I say.

WHAT?

"Don't tell me!" says Eric, closing his eyes and holding out the card.

I take the card.

"Now give it back to me."

I give it back to him. He puts the card on top of his head. He opens his eyes.

HI, GUYS.

"Your card is the Queen of Hearts!"

"Right," I say.

Eric bows.

"Great trick!" I applaud.

8

"It was nothing."

"We should put on a magic show," I say.

"Let's do it," answers Eric. He holds out the card to me again. "I'll teach you this trick. Pick a card." He smiles.

And so I am now . . . *the Great Hubini!*

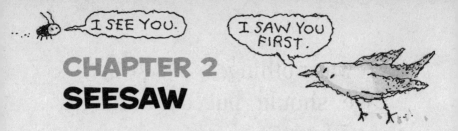

CHAPTER 2
SEESAW

"We're going to have to do other tricks. Do you know any others, Eric?" I ask.

"I saw one on TV where this magician sawed a lady in half."

"How did it turn out?"

"She was beside herself for a while, but they finally got their act together."

"Good," I say. "I'll saw you in half."

"No way. I'll saw *you* in half," says Eric.

"I said it first," I say.

"Well, I saw it first," says Eric.

"Looks like we're on a seesaw." I smile. "I think we need to find another victim . . . I mean assistant."

"Or a different trick," says Eric. "Let's go to the library. I bet Mrs. Beamster has a book full of magic tricks."

CHAPTER 3
HALF A FRIEND IS BETTER THAN NONE

At the library, Mrs. Beamster has exactly what we need. She walks over to the shelf and pulls out a book called *1,000 Magic Tricks You Can Do*.

We applaud.

She bows.

Eric and I sit at a table and open the book. Eric reads out loud.

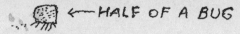 ←—HALF OF A BUG

"Chapter One. Things you will need: a magician's cape."

"I have a green towel," I say.

"Good," says Eric. "Number two: a magician's cap."

"I have a baseball cap," I say.

PERFECT!

1,000 MAGIC TRICKS YOU CAN DO

"Good," smiles Eric. "We'll also need a magician's assistant."

"We have Tailspin," I say.

"I think we need a real person," says Eric.

"And we'll have to get some insurance. Just in case we saw someone in half and can't put them back together again."

"Or if we make someone disappear and can't find them," says Eric.

Just then Doris walks into the library. Eric waves her over.

"Yes?" she asks.

"How would you like to be in a magic show?" I ask.

"Shush!" warns Mrs. Beamster.

16

HAVE YOU SEEN WENDELL?

HE DISAPPEARED.

"How would you like to be in a magic show?" Eric whispers.

"What do I have to do?" whispers Doris.

"Nothing," I whisper. "We'll do it all."

WHISPERING ONLY ON THIS PAGE.

OK.

"And what do YOU DO?" she asks, folding her arms.

"We put you in a box, we make you disappear, we saw you in half—Doris, come back!" Eric calls to her while she walks away.

"Shush!" says Mrs. Beamster with her finger over her lips.

"Oh well, we'll have to find another assistant," whispers Eric.

"There's always Tailspin," I smile.

NOT AMUSED

THIS IS A LIBRARY.

19

CHAPTER 4
VOLUN-TEARS

Eric and I ask everyone in school to be our assistant. Eric gets more and more excited each time he asks.

"We wrap you in chains. We put you in water. We make you float up to the ceiling . . ."

ERIC, BE QUIET.

HUH?

WHAT?

Nobody wants to be our assistant.

On the school bus ride home, Eric looks at me. I know what he is going to say.

"No way!" I answer before he opens his mouth. "I'm the magician, not the assistant."

"Then we still have Tailspin," he mumbles.

DO NOT
TOUCH ➔

21

Tailspin starts wagging his tail. "See, he already does tricks," I say.

"He's short," says Eric.
"So are we."
"Let's try it," says Eric.
We all walk to my house.

WOW!

CHAPTER 5
TEACHING A NEW DOG OLD TRICKS

"Mom, do you have a box?" I shout from the living room.

"How big?" she asks.

"Big enough for Tailspin," says Eric.

"What are you boys up to?"

"Magic," I answer.

"We're putting on a magic show," says Eric.

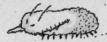

"I'm the *Great Hubini*," I bow, "and this is *Eric the Great*."

"Nice to meet you. And who is Tailspin?" Mom asks.

"Our assistant," we both answer.

"So, Mom, do you have a box?"

"All I have is the box my computer came in."

"It'll do," I say.

"We'll have to fix it up," says Eric.

SPARKLES→

TAPE →

We spend the afternoon covering it with red paper and sticking on sparkles.

"Cool," says Eric, stepping back to admire our work. "Let's get Tailspin."

GLUE

MOM, THANKS FOR THE SPARKLES.

DULL SCISSORS

BOX

RUBBER FROG

RED CHRISTMAS WRAPPING PAPER

27

CAN I ASSIST YOU?

NO, I CAN EAT YOU BY MYSELF.

We get Tailspin and put him in the box. He jumps out. We put him in again. He jumps out. We put him in a third time and quickly close the lid. He jumps around so much, the box shakes and all the sparkles come off.

"Oh well," I sigh. "Maybe we don't need an assistant."

"All right, all right," says Eric. "I'll be the assistant."

"Eric, this is a great sacrifice, a grand gesture, a noble deed."

"All right, all right," says Eric. "Let's get started."

SPARKLES

"First, we have to borrow a tutu from Doris—

"Eric, Eric, come back!"

All I hear is the door slam. I look at all the sparkles on the floor. Our magic show is falling apart before it's even started.

CHAPTER 6
THE REAL THING

That night I see the Great Gizmo on television. He has a real magician's cape, a real magician's cap, and a real assistant. Wow! He puts his assistant in a box and all the sparkles don't fall off. He sticks swords in the box. He makes her disappear. He even saws her in half and when she bows she stays together.

"Time for bed, Hubini," says Mom.

"It's just Hubie," I say, clicking off the television. "Just Hubie."

CHAPTER 7
STAGE FRIGHT

I lie in bed, but I can't fall asleep. I keep thinking about Saturday and all the things that can go wrong.

What if no one shows up?
What if everyone shows up? The whole school! Hundreds of kids looking at me.
Pressure!

What if I forget the jokes?

What if I remember the jokes and no one laughs?

What if I can't find an assistant? Will I have to cut myself in half?

What if the tricks don't work?

What if they work and nobody is amazed?

What if I throw up?

What if they throw up?

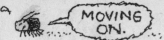

MOVING ON.

I'm sorry I started this whole thing.

I think *THIS IS GOING TO BE A DISASTER* as I fall asleep.

34

CHAPTER 8
BREAK A LEG

"I, DON'T HAVE A LEG TO BREAK."

I'm on a huge stage. Thousands of eyes are looking at me.

"For my next trick, I will pull a person out of a hat."

I pull off my baseball cap.

"Ta-daa!"

The whole crowd boos!

"I'm a person!" I say.

"We want our money back!" the audience shouts.

"For my next amazing feat of prestidigitation—"

"What's that?" the audience yells.

"It means 'magic trick,'" I explain.

"Why didn't you just say that?"
they shout.

Tough crowd, I think.

"I will now cut myself in half,"
I say.

The audience grows quiet in
anticipation.

I whip out the school yearbook
and a pair of scissors and cut my
photo in half.

PATHETIC!

TERRIBLE!

MOO.

YOU STINK.

YOU'RE A JOKE.

BOO!

"Boo! We want our money back!"

There's no pleasing some people, even in a dream.

CHAPTER 9
THREE'S A CROWD

SUNNY DAY →

PENNY.

YES, HUBIE.

The next morning, I sit next to Penny on the school bus.

"Did you see the Great Gizmo on television last night?"

"I did!" she says.

"Did you see his assistant?"

"I did."

TUMMY · YUMMY

"Wasn't it cool how she was onstage?" I ask.

"It was."

"I'm a magician," I say.

"You are?" asks Penny.

"And I'm doing a magic show on Saturday."

"Are you?" asks Penny.

"Would you like to be my assistant?"

"Well, maybe," she exclaims.

"I thought you wanted *me* to be your assistant," says Doris from across the aisle.

"Yesterday you asked *ME* to be your assistant," says Eric from behind us.

TWEET.

TREET →

41

"Mind your own business," says Penny.

"He asked me first," insists Doris.

"He asked me second," says Eric.

"He asked me most recent," says Penny.

"Don't fight," I say. "You can all be my assistants."

CHAPTER 10
TRICKED OUT

Now I have three assistants and no tricks.

After I get home from school, I empty out my piggy bank.

I have exactly $1.97. How could my piggy bank always only have $1.97 in it? Maybe it's a magic piggy bank. It will have to do.

SHAKE
SHAKE
SHAKE

IS THAT ALL?

CREEPY.

PIGGY BANK

COINS →

I get on my bike and ride over to the magic store. There is a picture of the Great Gizmo in the window. I go in and look around.

There are real magician's capes with red silk linings and real magician's caps that look like Abe Lincoln's. There are hoops, balls, and scarves of every color. There are wands, and cards, and magic boxes.

"Can I help you?" asks the man standing behind the counter.

"I'm a magician," I say.

"Good," says the man.

"I want to buy a trick."

"Good," says the man. "How much do you want to spend?"

"A dollar ninety-seven," I answer, holding out my money.

"Well," says the man, "I'll give you one trick for nothing."

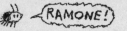

"Which one is that?"

"I'll show you how to vanish," he says, walking to the door.

"How do you do that?"

He opens the door.

"Disappear!" he says, pointing to the street.

I walk out. He closes the door.

Now I know one trick, but that's not enough to do a whole show. I guess I'll have to make up my own.

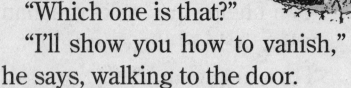

CHAPTER 11
HOMEGROWN MAGIC

When I get home, Mom is making dinner. I see a big spoon on the counter. It would make a good wand, so I pick it up.

I look in the closet. My green towel will make a good cape.

I find some black cardboard, roll it into a tube, and tape it. Voilà! A cap.

THE GREAT → HUBINI

TA-DA!

47

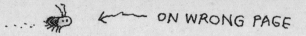

I'm batting three for three until Mom has to stir the soup. She takes the spoon back but says I can use the flyswatter. Oh well, nothing's perfect.

I still don't have any tricks.

BORING.

I search the internet for "magic tricks." There are lots of them.

"Water into ice."

No big deal. That happens every winter.

SKATES

ICE

← FROG

TOAD →

"Pencil through a baggie filled with water."

Could be messy.

Lots of tricks where you have to cut and glue stuff . . . too much trouble.

Then I see it.

"The unbreakable egg."

All you do is press on the ends of an egg as hard as you can . . . and it won't break.

That's it!

PROFESSIONAL WRESTLER ⟶

SQUEEZING EGG

"Mom, could I have an egg?"

"What for, Hubie?"

"For my trick, Mom."

"What trick, Hubie?"

"It's one of the greatest secrets of the universe, Mom."

"Here, Hubie. Don't make a mess."

THANKS, MOM.

CAN I HAVE BACON?

CHAPTER 12
STAGE-STRUCK

I have one trick and Saturday is quickly approaching. My three assistants made posters and put them up all over school.

After school, Eric helps me make a stage by turning over the kiddie pool. We string a bedsheet between two trees for a curtain. It all looks pretty professional. We set up ten folding chairs. We are optimistic about attendance.

That night I invent a few more tricks to round out the show.

CHAPTER 13
SHOWTIME

Saturday arrives and I have butterflies in my stomach. If I could cough them out, it would be a good trick.

I'm ready as the crowd starts to file in . . .

Well, it isn't exactly a crowd.

There's Freddy, who is in charge of snacks. He's selling popcorn.

Derek and Randy both come to see the show.

My three assistants look great. They're all wearing tutus . . . including Eric.

Mom comes out of the house to fill up the audience, but then she goes back inside. Tailspin sits, wagging his tail in eager anticipation.

CLAP!
CLAP!
CLAP!

POPCORN
↓

SNACKS

"TA-DA!"

Eric steps out from behind the curtain. Everyone cheers.

"Today, we are going to present the most amazing feats of magic ever seen in this backyard."

HUBIE

THANK YOU, THANK YOU VERY MUCH.

RACCOON

RIBBIT.

CLAP! CLAP!

"TA-DA-TA-DA!"

Penny and Doris open the curtain. There I stand in my cape and cap, with a cotton beard taped to my chin. I throw back my cape and take off my cap. The brim comes loose and the cardboard unrolls. Everyone applauds.

CLAP! CLAP!

"Thank you . . . for my first trick, I will press on this egg as hard as I can and it will NOT break!"

I hold up the egg between my two magic hands and press as hard as I can.

The egg doesn't break.

"Big deal!" says Randy, coming up onstage and grabbing the egg.

CLAP! CLAP!

CLAP!

"It's hard-boiled!"

"It's not hard-boiled," I shout.

"It is!"

"Is not!"

Randy grabs the egg and presses on the sides. The egg breaks all over his shirt.

"It's not!" he says, egg dripping from both hands.

"We have just demonstrated how to make an omelet!"

Mom comes out again. "Are you kids making a mess?"

Some days, magic can be tragic.

"For my last and final trick, I will make the sun disappear."

"Oh yeah," snickers Derek.

"Into thin air," I say.

"Go ahead," chides Derek.

"Be patient," I say. "This trick takes a little time."

Everyone sits very still, waiting patiently. I wave the flyswatter. It slowly gets darker.

"Wow!" says Derek. "You're doing it!"

"Now that the sun's gone down, do you want the cookies?" shouts Mom from the house.

"Mom! You're giving away the trick!"

Everyone applauds in the dark.

"Isn't there something else we can do?" ask Penny and Doris.

"Close the curtain," I sigh.

FLYSWATTER

I'M NOT A FLY!!

BOYBUG →

CHAPTER 14
HAPPY ENDING

We all have cookies and milk and leftover popcorn in the house. Then we sit around the living room and watch a movie.

WOW!

"For my final trick, I will make everyone's money return," I say.

They all cheer!

I give everyone back their fifty cents and they all go home happy.

Ya know, all in all, it was a pretty magical evening.

EGG MAGIC REVEALED

Eggs are strong, even though we think of them as fragile. The curved structure at the top of the egg creates an arch, one of the strongest designs in nature. Applying pressure at the top and bottom spreads the force evenly over the shell as you push on the egg. Applying a sharp force to the side will cause it to break, which is why we usually tap the egg on the side of a bowl.

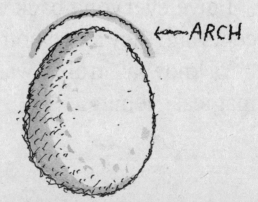

←—ARCH